Do Your ABC's, Little Brown Bear

JONATHAN LONDON

illustrated by **MARGIE MOORE**

PUFFIN BOOKS

PUFFIN BOOKS
Published by the Penguin Group
Penguin Young Readers Group, 345 Hudson Street, New York, New York 10014, U.S.A.
Penguin Group (Canada), 90 Eglinton Avenue East, Suite 700, Toronto, Ontario, Canada M4P 2Y3
(a division of Pearson Penguin Canada Inc.)
Penguin Books Ltd, 80 Strand, London WC2R 0RL, England
Penguin Ireland, 25 St Stephen's Green, Dublin 2, Ireland
(a division of Penguin Books Ltd)
Penguin Group (Australia), 250 Camberwell Road, Camberwell, Victoria 3124, Australia
(a division of Pearson Australia Group Pty Ltd)
Penguin Books India Pvt Ltd, 11 Community Centre, Panchsheel Park, New Delhi - 110 017, India
Penguin Group (NZ), Cnr Airborne and Rosedale Roads, Albany, Auckland 1310,
New Zealand (a division of Pearson New Zealand Ltd)
Penguin Books (South Africa) (Pty) Ltd, 24 Sturdee Avenue, Rosebank, Johannesburg 2196, South Africa

Registered Offices: Penguin Books Ltd, 80 Strand, London WC2R 0RL, England

First published in the United States of America by Dutton Children's Books,
a division of Penguin Young Readers Group, 2005
Published by Puffin Books, a division of Penguin Young Readers Group, 2007

1 3 5 7 9 10 8 6 4 2

Text copyright © Jonathan London, 2005
Illustrations copyright © Margie Moore, 2005
All rights reserved
CIP Data is available.

ISBN 978-0-14-240713-4

Manufactured in China

For Sean and Aaron

J.L.

For my mother

M.M.

Papa Brown Bear and Little Brown Bear
were playing in a meadow in Bear Valley.
"What do you want to do now?" asked Little Brown Bear.
"I'd like you," said Papa Brown Bear, "to do your ABC's."

"Hurray!" said Little Brown Bear.

He reached up and plucked fruit from a branch.

"A is for Apple!" he said.

"Good choice!" said Papa Brown Bear.

"What comes next?"

"**B** is for Ball!" said Little Brown Bear.

He threw a baseball smack into Papa's nose—bonk!

"You're supposed to catch it," said Little Brown Bear.
"C is for Catch! Now throw it to me, Papa!"

Papa Brown Bear tossed the ball, and . . .
"Yippee! I caught it!" yelled Little Brown Bear.

He hopped and skipped.
"D is for Dance!" said Little Brown Bear.
Little Brown Bear and Papa Brown Bear
did a silly dance in the meadow.

"I'm hungry," said Little Brown Bear.

"Why don't you eat your apple?" said Papa Brown Bear.

"E is for Eat!" said Little Brown Bear. "Yum!"

"All done," he said. "Let's take this shortcut—
because **F** is for Fence!"
Up and over they went.

"**G** is for Grass! Grass fight!" yelled Little Brown Bear.
He threw a pawful at Papa Brown Bear.
"Gotcha!" said Papa Brown Bear,
throwing a pawful back.

"Watch me!" said Little Brown Bear.
"I'm going to hit this ball,
because **H** is for Hit!" Whack!
They chased the ball toward the stream.

"I is for Icy!" said Little Brown Bear
when he and Papa sat down by the stream.
"This water is too cold for my toes!"
"But it's great for drinking! Yum!" Papa Brown Bear slurped.

"J is for Joke!" Little Brown Bear said.

"I know a good one! What kind of shoes does a bear wear?"

"I give up," said Papa.

"Bears don't wear shoes," said Little Brown Bear.

"They go Bear-footed!"

Papa Brown Bear laughed.

"The wind is blowing hard!" said Papa Brown Bear.
"K is for Kite!" said Little Brown Bear. "Let's go fly mine!"
And they ran to the open field
and sailed it high in the breeze.

When he got tired of running, Little Brown Bear said,
"L is for Lap!" and he climbed into Papa's lap.
"Tell me a story, Papa!"
Papa Brown Bear told him his favorite tale.

"**M** is for More! Tell me another story!"
cried Little Brown Bear.
"One is enough for now," said Papa Brown Bear.
"Let's go play in the forest."

"N is for Nuts!" said Little Brown Bear.
"Look at all the acorns on the ground!"
Little Brown Bear and Papa Brown Bear
found the perfect acorns for making
acorn-hat whistles. Tweet! Tweet!

"**O** is for Oak tree!" said Little Brown Bear.
"I'm going to climb to the top!"
When he reached the highest branch,
Papa Brown Bear asked,
"What can you see from up there?"

"**P** is for Pond!" said Little Brown Bear.
"I can see the pond across the meadow!"

Little Brown Bear climbed down to the ground
and said, "Let's go to the pond!"
On the way there, Papa Brown Bear pointed at a bird
and said, "Hush!"
"Q is for Quiet!" said Little Brown Bear
in his softest voice.

The quail fluttered away, and Little Brown Bear said,
"**R** is for Race! Betcha can't catch me!"
he hollered as they ran to the pond.

"S is for Swim!" he said. Splash! Splash! Splash!
Papa jumped in after him. "Cannonball!" he yelled.
Splash!

"**T** is for Towel!" said Little Brown Bear
as Papa Brown Bear wrapped him snug and warm.
"It's going to rain!" said Papa Brown Bear.
"Let's make a dash for it!"

"Up!" said Little Brown Bear. "U is for Up!"
And Papa Brown Bear gave him a piggyback ride
all the way home in the rain.

After supper, Papa Brown Bear said, "Time for bed!"

"V is for Vroom!" said Little Brown Bear.

He spread his arms like airplane wings
and sped around the room.

"Come back, you little rascal!" hollered Papa.

"W is for Wrestle!" cried Little Brown Bear,
and he made a flying tackle.
"Give up?" asked Little Brown Bear,
pinning Papa down.
"I give up!" said Papa Brown Bear.

"Now off to bed!" he said.

"Not before we finish the ABC's!"
said Little Brown Bear.

"But I don't know any X words."

"There's a toy in the corner that begins with X," said Papa.

"Oh yeah! X is for Xylophone!"

Papa Brown Bear yawned while Little Brown Bear

banged on the xylophone.

"Y is for Yawn!" Little Brown Bear said,

and his mouth stretched wide open.

Papa Brown Bear helped him into his pajamas.

"And **Z** is for . . ." said Little Brown Bear.

"Zip it!" Papa interrupted. "I'm bushed! Now go to bed!"

"Okay, Papa. Good night!" said Little Brown Bear.

"Good night," said Papa Brown Bear.

And Little Brown Bear climbed into bed . . .

and zipped off to sleep.